A Note to Parents and Caregivers:

Read-it! Readers are for children who are just starting on the amazing road to reading. These beautiful books support both the acquisition of reading skills and the love of books.

The PURPLE LEVEL presents basic topics and objects using high frequency words and simple language patterns.

The RED LEVEL presents familiar topics using common words and repeating sentence patterns.

The BLUE LEVEL presents new ideas using a larger vocabulary and varied sentence structure.

The YELLOW LEVEL presents more challenging ideas, a broad vocabulary, and wide variety in sentence structure.

The GREEN LEVEL presents more complex ideas, an extended vocabulary range, and expanded language structures.

The ORANGE LEVEL presents a wide range of ideas and concepts using challenging vocabulary and complex language structures.

When sharing a book with your child, read in short stretches, pausing often to talk about the pictures. Have your child turn the pages and point to the pictures and familiar words. And be sure to reread favorite stories or parts of stories.

There is no right or wrong way to share books with children. Find time to read with your child, and pass on the legacy of literacy.

Adria F. Klein, Ph.D.
Professor Emeritus
California State University
San Bernardino, California

Editor: Patricia Stockland
Storyboarder: Amy Bailey Muehlenhardt
Page Production: Melissa Kes/JoAnne Nelson/Tracy Davies
Art Director: Keith Griffin
Managing Editor: Catherine Neitge
The illustrations in this book were rendered in acrylic.

Picture Window Books
5115 Excelsior Boulevard
Suite 232
Minneapolis, MN 55416
877-845-8392
www.picturewindowbooks.com

Printed in the United States of America.

Library of Congress Cataloging-in-Publication Data
Blair, Eric.
Annie Oakley, Sharp Shooter / by Eric Blair ; illustrated by Micah Chambers-Goldberg.
p. cm.—(Read-it! readers: tall tales)
ISBN 1-4048-0970-8 (hardcover)
1. Oakley, Annie, 1860-1926—Juvenile literature. 2. Shooters of firearms—United States
—Biography—Juvenile literature. 3. Entertainers—United States—Biography—Juvenile
literature. I. Chambers-Goldberg, Micah, ill. II. Title. III. Read-it! readers tall tales.
GV1157.O3B53 2004
799.3'092—dc22   2004018436

Annie Oakley, Sharp Shooter

By Eric Blair

Illustrated by Micah Chambers-Goldberg

Special thanks to our advisers for their expertise:

Adria F. Klein, Ph.D.
Professor Emeritus, California State University
San Bernardino, California

Susan Kesselring, M.A.
Literacy Educator
Rosemount-Apple Valley-Eagan (Minnesota) School District

PICTURE WINDOW BOOKS
Minneapolis, Minnesota

When little Annie Oakley was five,
her father died.

To help feed her family, Annie learned to shoot. She may have been tiny, but she had extremely good eyesight.

Chefs at hotels and restaurants
bought the animals she shot.
Soon, Annie earned so much
money that she bought her
mother a farm.

When Annie was only sixteen, she entered a shooting contest with Frank Butler, a famous marksman.

Frank laughed at the tiny girl,
but Annie shot all twenty-five targets.
Frank missed one. Frank lost the
contest, but he won Annie's heart.
Soon, they were married.

13

14

Frank and Annie became business partners, too. They did trick shooting at shows.

People came from all over to see Annie's amazing skills.

16

Annie and Frank had a dog named Dave. One of Annie's sharp-shooting tricks was to shoot an apple off Dave's head. He was always safe.

Annie could also shoot backwards and hit moving targets. She watched the targets through a handheld mirror.

Another trick Annie liked was to shoot a dime tossed into the air.

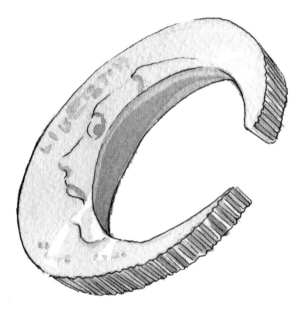

Sometimes, Annie even shot while riding a horse!

Annie's favorite trick was to shoot at a playing card.

She would shoot six holes in the
falling card before it
hit the ground.

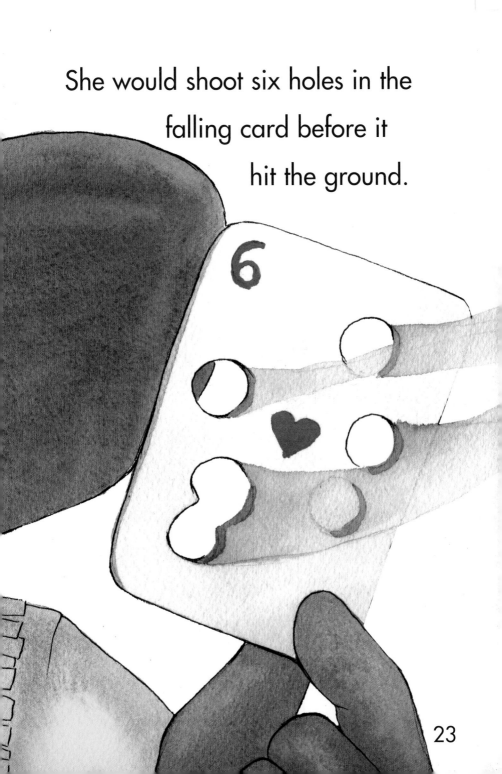

Annie had great tricks and great friends. She was even friends with the famous Sioux Indian Chief Sitting Bull. He called her "Little Sure Shot."

25

After a while, Annie joined the most famous show of them all: Buffalo Bill's Wild West Show. Annie Oakley became a star.

Annie toured the whole world with Buffalo Bill's Wild West Show.

The tours made Annie rich
and famous.

Annie was generous with her money. Once, she bought ice cream for all the kids in Texas.

Annie Oakley was always tiny, but she had a huge heart—and a huge stomach!

More *Read-it!* Readers

Bright pictures and fun stories help you practice your reading skills. Look for more books at your level.

TALL TALES

Annie Oakley, Sharp Shooter by Eric Blair

John Henry by Christianne C. Jones

Johnny Appleseed by Eric Blair

The Legend of Daniel Boone by Eric Blair

Paul Bunyan by Eric Blair

Pecos Bill by Eric Blair

Looking for a specific title or level? A complete list of *Read-it!* Readers is available on our Web site: *www.picturewindowbooks.com*